KU-239-194

The BRAVE Little OWL

WRITTEN BY GILL DAVIES   ILLUSTRATIONS BY DICK TWINNEY

mustard

Little Owl fluffs up his soft, furry feathers.

His bright round eyes peep out of the nest.
Then he squeaks. He squeaks because
he is afraid of the dark outside.

The fox cubs laugh as they play below.
"Owls are meant to like night-time best," they tease.

"What a funny little owl!" laugh the squirrels.

"An odd little owl," giggle the moths.

"A very strange owl," agree the rabbits, "to be
frightened of the dark."

Mother Owl tries to comfort Little Owl.
"Be brave, Little Owl," she says.
"Look at the stars. See how beautiful they are."

"Be brave, Little Owl. Look at the moon.
See how big and golden it is," says Father Owl.

But Little Owl buries his head under his wing.

"Be brave, Little Owl. Look at the velvet sky.
See how deep and blue it is!" call the deer.
Their antlers glisten in the moonlight.
But still Little Owl hides. He sinks his head
deeper into his feathers.
He squeezes his eyes tightly shut.

It is time for Little Owl to learn to fly.

He sits on the branches of the tree with the other baby owls in a wobbling row.

The breeze blows their feathers and the leaves whisper. The other forest creatures come to watch.

Little Owl is terrified. He closes his eyes.
Then, suddenly, he hears a night bird singing.

The music is beautiful.
He hears a waterfall splashing.

The sound is exciting.
He wants to hear more and he forgets to be afraid.

All the forest animals cheer!

Little Owl opens his big round eyes even wider.
He flies above the forest.
He flies across the golden moon.
He flies past the sparkling, glittering stars.

Brave Little Owl sees that the night is not dark after all.

Brave Little Owl sees how bright the night is.
It is beautiful!
"Tu-whit tu-whoo," sings Brave Little Owl,
and he flies off into the shining, silver night.

This is a Mustard Book
Mustard is an imprint of Parragon

Parragon,

Queen Street House,

4 Queen Street, Bath BA1 1HE

Produced by the Templar Company plc,

Pippbrook Mill, London Road, Dorking, Surrey RH4 1JE

Copyright © 1999 by the Templar Company plc

All rights reserved.

ISBN 1-84164-048-4

Designed by Hayley Bebb
Edited by Dugald Steer

Printed in Singapore